Virtual Apprentice

FBI AGENT

By Gail Karlitz

Ferguson

An imprint of Infobase Publishing

Virtual Apprentice: FBI Agent

Ferguson
An imprint of Infobase Publishing
132 West 31st Street
New York, NY 10001

Library of Congress Cataloging-in-Publication Data

Karlitz, Gail.
  Virtual apprentice : FBI agent / Gail Karlitz.
      p. cm.
  Includes index.
  ISBN 978-0-8160-6758-9 (hc : alk. paper) 1. United States. Federal Bureau of Investigation—Juvenile literature. 2. United States. Federal Bureau of Investigation—Vocational guidance. 3. Law enforcement—United States—Juvenile literature. 4. Criminal investiga-tion—United States—Juvenile literature. I. Title.
  HV8144.F43K37 2007
  363.25023'73—dc22

                              2006036568

Ferguson books are available at special discounts when purchased in bulk quantities for businesses, associations, institutions, or sales promotions. Please call our Special Sales Department in New York at (212) 967-8800 or (800) 322-8755.

You can find Ferguson on the World Wide Web at http://www.fergpubco.com

Produced by Bright Futures Press (http://www.brightfuturespress.com)
Series created by Diane Lindsey Reeves
Interior design by Tom Carling, carlingdesign.com
Cover design by Salvatore Luongo

Photo Credits: Table of Contents Mark Peterson/CORBIS; Page 5 Butch Dill/epa/CORBIS; Page 7 Bettmann/CORBIS; Page 10 Bettmann/CORBIS; Page 13 Shootalot/Dreamstime.com; Page 15 Federal Bureau of Investigation, Office of Public Affairs; Page 18 Federal Bureau of Investigation, Office of Public Affairs; Page 23 Federal Bureau of Investigation, Office of Public Affairs; Page 26 Amy Toensing/Sygma/Corbis: Page 30 Avatarfoto/Dreamstime.com; Page 33 Greg Smith/CORBIS; Page 38 Mark Peterson/CORBIS.

Note to Readers: Please note that every effort was made to include accurate Web site addresses for kid-friendly resources listed throughout this book. However, Web site content and addresses change often and the author and publisher of this book cannot be held accountable for any inappropriate material that may appear on these Web sites. In the interest of keeping your online exploration safe and appropriate, we strongly suggest that all Internet searches be conducted under the supervision of a parent or other trusted adult.

CONTENTS

The Wonderful World of FBI Agents

"Freeze! FBI! Drop your weapon!"

You've seen that scene a hundred times in movies and on television. The FBI agents, wearing their bulletproof FBI vests, barge into a house (or store, or apartment, or warehouse) where they find the kidnappers (or bank robbers, or drug dealers, or gang members). The bad guys fight back, but they are no match for the FBI agents, who subdue them and put them away where they can never hurt anyone again.

Can you see yourself doing something like that? Or what about working in a crime lab and finding the clue that stops a serial killer before he strikes again? Can you imagine what it would be like to return a kidnapped child to his or her parents? Or to stop an evil terrorist attack?

You may have just what it takes to do these things, even if you're not the big, bad, risk-taking hero type. FBI agents specialize in so many different kinds of work. See if there's a place in the FBI that is just right for you.

What is it really like to be an FBI agent? Read on, and find out about

• how and why the FBI got started

• what an FBI agent might do on a typical day

• the amazing technologies that help FBI agents crack even the toughest cases

• what it takes to become an FBI agent

• the people who help agents do their jobs

• what real agents have to say when kids like you ask them what it's *really* like to be an FBI agent

And while you're at it, do a few reality checks, investigate some resources, and test your skill at some pop quizzes. Ready for more? Bring on the virtual FBI-agent-for-a-day experience and find out for yourself what it's really like to be an FBI agent. You'll be amazed to discover all the things you can do in the FBI.

Are you ready to help solve the crime?

CHAPTER 1

The FBI: Then and Now

CHECK IT OUT

Learn more about the gangsters of the lawless years, including what they did and how the FBI captured them: http://www.fbi .gov/libref/historic/ famcases/famcases .htm.

"Don't shoot, G-men! Don't shoot!"

No… that's not just a line from an old movie. It's one version of the legend of how "Machine Gun" Kelly, one of the most notorious mobsters of the 1920s and 1930s, was captured by Memphis police and federal agents. "Machine Gun" Kelly was obviously a little surprised when armed police and FBI agents stormed into a house and captured him in 1933.

John Dillinger, then known as "public enemy number one," was equally surprised when, in 1934, he came out of a Chicago movie theater to find himself surrounded by FBI agents. Three of the agents shot him dead on the street.

Kelly and Dillinger were just two of the mobsters and gangsters who flourished in the 1920s and 1930s, a period often called the "lawless years." In those days, *gangster* referred to members of criminal gangs, not the hip-hop music and styles the word is used for today. And, in those days, the FBI was known as the Bureau of Investigation. The organization had several different names before it officially became the Federal Bureau of Investigation in 1935.

There are many different versions of stories about the gangsters of those years. One lasting result of the "Machine

> # "The cure for crime is not the electric chair, but the high chair."
>
> —J. EDGAR HOOVER, FIRST FBI DIRECTOR

Gun" Kelly story is that the term *G-Man*, which had long been a slang word for any government agent, soon came to stand only for the heroic FBI agents who tracked down criminals and brought them to justice.

The Lawless Years

Some of the more powerful gangsters of that time were colorful characters, and the public knew about them in the same way as we know about some of the organized crime figures of today. Those well-known gangsters included Al Capone (known as "Scarface"), Charles "Pretty Boy" Floyd, Lester "Baby Face" Nelson, Jack "Legs" Diamond, and Charlie "Lucky" Luciano. Fortunately, many of the famous, as well as the lesser known, gangsters had their careers cut short through the work of the FBI.

The gangsters rose to power with Prohibition, a period from 1920 to 1933 when the U.S. government outlawed the manufacture, sale, and transportation of alcohol. Many people did not support Prohibition and refused to give up their liquor. Criminals saw this as a golden opportunity. They made their own alcohol and smuggled it into this country from Canada and Mexico, where it was legal to make it.

The illegal alcohol business was huge, and it required a lot of workers for manufacturing

Gangster John Dillinger, once known as "public enemy number one."

and distribution. Illegal alcohol was also extremely profitable. Some of the more ambitious criminals realized that if they organized their activities to work in the style of legitimate companies it would be easier to get the workers they needed and to force their competitors out of business.

The gangsters were very serious about getting rid of their competitors. For example, the gang run by Al Capone was not happy that "Bugs" Moran's gang was doing business in the area that they had claimed for themselves. Their solution to this problem came to be known as the famous St. Valentine's Day Massacre of 1929. Al Capone's men, disguised as police officers, lured seven members of Moran's gang into a garage and gunned them down in cold blood.

Gangsters didn't limit themselves to crimes involving alcohol. John Dillinger earned his standing as "public enemy number one" in part by using his gang to rob five banks in less than four months. Each time Dillinger and his gang were captured for a crime, they escaped from jail. In the process they shot and killed police officers, prison guards, a sheriff, and an FBI agent. They took hostages, stole weapons and bulletproof vests from three different police departments, and used a sheriff's car to escape. Once Dillinger crossed state lines in the stolen car, FBI agents had the authority to go after him, which they promptly did.

There were many gangsters who were just a little too slick for the local police. Some moved to another state, counting on the fact that the police didn't have enough information to track them down. The FBI, however, had more sophisticated investigation methods, as well as the authority to track gangsters whose criminal activities involved more than one state. So FBI

Who Does What?

The FBI is not the only agency that protects America and its citizens.

The Secret Service, for example, provides security for the president of the United States and for presidential candidates. It also investigates counterfeiting. The Central Intelligence Agency (CIA) collects information regarding citizens of foreign countries who may be spying on us here or in their own countries.

See what else these agencies do at their Web sites:

➤ Central Intelligence Agency https://www.cia.gov/kids-page/index.html

➤ Secret Service http://www.secretservice.gov/kids_faq.shtml

➤ Department of Justice http://www.usdoj.gov/usao/eousa/kidspage/index.html

agents went after criminals who thought they were safe when they were "on the lam."

How It All Started

Although the FBI established its reputation during those lawless years, the agency actually began in 1908. Before that, most crimes were investigated at the state or local level. Crimes committed on federal property or crimes that violated a federal law, however, were the responsibility of the attorney general (the country's top lawyer, law enforcement officer, and head of the Department of Justice). Because the attorney general did not have anyone to work on these crimes, he would hire private detectives or use investigators from other agencies, such as the Secret Service.

In 1908, Congress ruled that the federal government could no longer use Secret Service agents. Attorney General Charles Bonaparte, with the permission of President Theodore Roosevelt, created a "bureau" of 34 special agents to work for the Department of Justice. Even though the group didn't have an official name, these former detectives and Secret Service agents were the first FBI agents.

When the United States entered World War I in 1917, the FBI (then called the Bureau of Investigation) looked for spies and people who did not register for military service as they were required to do. The bureau's responsibility was soon increased to include motor vehicle thefts and crimes that affected more than one state. As transportation and communication became easier, more and more criminals crossed state lines, and by the 1920s, the bureau had grown to 300 special agents and 300 support employees, with field offices set up around the country.

During and following World War II, the FBI increased its size even more and focused its resources on monitoring America's enemies with investigations to keep its foes from learning national secrets. When the United States became the first nation to develop nuclear weapons, it became especially important to make sure foreign spies did not learn how these weapons were made.

After a while, the bureau's priorities moved back to crime, which remained the priority until 1993. Between 1993 and 1996, terrorism was a big issue for the United States, and the FBI solved

FUN FACTOID

The FBI is usually looking for 12,000 different criminals at any one time. Not all of them qualify for the Ten Most Wanted list.

J. Edgar Hoover (right) was the FBI director under eight U.S. presidents, including John Kennedy.

several important cases, including the 1993 bombing of the World Trade Center in New York, the bombing of the Alfred P. Murrah Federal Building in Oklahoma City in 1995, and the Unabomber, who terrorized America for 18 years by sending mail bombs (packages that explode when opened) to professors and scientists.

J. Edgar Hoover

Between 1924 and 1972, the biggest influence on the FBI's priorities and organization was J. Edgar Hoover, who served as FBI director for 48 years. When he first took over leadership of the FBI, Hoover initiated many changes to make the organization more professional, including firing agents he considered unqualified. He ordered background checks, interviews, and physical tests for all new agents. He required new agents to have legal or accounting backgrounds. And, because Hoover wanted agents to look professional, he insisted that they always wear a dark suit, a white shirt, and a hat. Hoover's ideas helped make the FBI the most professional law enforcement agency in the world. Accomplishments during his administration include the following:

• A centralized fingerprint file was begun at the Identification Division (1925).

• The FBI Technical Laboratory was created (1932). Originally set up for research purposes, the FBI crime lab is now the most sophisticated forensic laboratory in the world. It is located in Quantico, Virginia, and employs nearly 700 specially trained scientists. These scientists work around the clock to carry out more than one million investigations each year for state and local authorities as well as for the FBI itself.

• A formal training course for new agents was developed, and the National Police Academy was established (1935). Today the academy, also located in Quantico, offers training to the highest qualified personnel from law enforcement agencies around the country.

J. Edgar Hoover was a controversial figure. He has been criticized for some of his goals and some of his methods were highly questionable. But, even his critics have to agree that he brought about the professionalism that the bureau is known for today.

Today's FBI

Today, the FBI is concerned with three major areas

- protecting the United States and its citizens from terrorism and foreign enemies

- fighting crime at the national, or federal, level

- helping other law enforcement agencies be more effective in their work

Spies, attacks, and war are some of the scariest things imaginable. The United States has been safer from these terrors than many other countries, in part because the FBI has been on the job. Today, the FBI remains the first line of defense against espionage (spies from other countries), sabotage (enemies destroying property or equipment to weaken the country), and terrorism (the use, or threat, of force or violence to achieve political objectives).

After the terrorist attacks of September 11, 2001, commonly called "9/11," the FBI began to change its organization to better protect the United States. In 2005, the FBI established its National Security Branch to combat these threats even more carefully and aggressively.

The National Security Branch unites four divisions to make the most effective use of their different abilities and resources. The four divisions are

- Counterterrorism, which addresses the highest priority of the FBI: to protect the United States from terrorist attack.

- Counterintelligence refers to the FBI's second highest priority: to protect the United States against foreign intelligence

CHECK IT OUT

Ready for a Special Agent challenge? Go online to http://www.fbi.gov/kids/6th12th/sachallenge/sachallenge.htm and see how you do. Once you pass this hurdle, head over to http://www.fbi.gov/kids/games/games.htm for a little FBI-style fun and games.

operations and espionage. That means that the FBI acts to protect the secrets of the United States, whether those secrets are about political information, military operations or capabilities, or even the inventions and business plans of American companies.

• Intelligence refers to information about people or organizations. There are many ways to gather intelligence. Intelligence can be gathered through the Internet and through analysis of public information like newspapers, magazines, and legal documents. It can be gathered by talking to people, whether they are directly involved in an activity or are ordinary citizens who want to help with the FBI's mission. And finally, intelligence can be gathered through spying.

• Weapons of mass destruction (WMDs) are a very high priority of the National Security Branch. The goal of the Weapons of Mass Destruction Directorate is to link all intelligence and law enforcement operations in order to stop the spread of nuclear weapons and other weapons of mass destruction from country to country and to disrupt any attempts to use WMDs against the United States and its interests.

Crime Fighters

The FBI has the authority to investigate violations of more than 200 categories of federal law. They investigate all bank robberies, kidnappings, cybercrime, and "fugitives from justice" (people who leave a state to avoid getting arrested or going to court). The first step in solving any case is identifying the person who committed a crime. The next step is finding the criminal, which is not always easy. One tool that has helped the FBI catch some of the worst criminals is widespread publication of its Ten Most Wanted list.

The FBI Ten Most Wanted List

FIND OUT MORE

➤ Longest time on the list: Donald Eugene Webb was removed without being captured on March 31, 2007.

➤ Shortest time on the list: Billie Austin Bryant, who was captured just two hours after he was listed in 1969.

➤ Total number of women who have made the list: Eight as of June 2008.

➤ Osama Bin Laden has been on the list since 1999 for his alleged involvement in the 1998 bombing of the U.S. embassies in Kenya and Tanzania.

The J. Edgar Hoover building in Washington, D.C., is the main headquarters for the FBI.

How Does the FBI Do It All?

The FBI is responsible for protecting the security of the United States, for solving many types of crimes, and for providing state and local agencies with training, resources, and help on difficult cases. That's a lot of work! It takes a lot of organization, almost $6 billion, and more than 30,000 employees to get the job done.

Think you would like to be one of those employees? Keep reading to learn exactly what a "G-man" does and what it takes to be one.

CHAPTER 2

FBI Agent at Work

FUN FACTOID

Last year, the FBI investigated crimes involving more than 188,000 victims, including many children. The FBI's Office for Victim Assistance can ensure that victims receive the rights to which they are entitled and assistance to help them cope with the impact of crime and rebuild their lives. To find out more, check out the FBI's Victim Assistance program at http://www.fbi.gov/hq/cid/victimassist/home.htm.

On television, FBI agents solve major crimes in just one hour (minus time for commercials!). Real life crimes take a lot longer to solve, but an FBI agent's day is full of so many different activities that some days could easily translate into a month of television episodes.

One thing is sure—there are no typical days for FBI agents. There is not even a "typical workplace." Over the course of his or her career, a special agent may work at FBI headquarters in Washington, D.C., at one or more field offices or resident agencies, and even in another country.

For an FBI agent, every day is something new. And that's exactly what most agents love about their jobs. Put yourself in their shoes for a day to see what they mean.

It's 5:00 a.m., you're sound asleep, dreaming that a phone is ringing. Wait a sec… That's no dream. It's a call for you to come out to a crime scene. Pronto

No big surprise. Even though you're not "officially" due at your office until 9 a.m., emergency calls coming at strange hours are hardly unusual. You work on the drug crimes squad in your field office, and drug dealers do not exactly keep regular business hours.

> ## "Each day is different. I start my day knowing that 'today could be the day.'"
> ### —IMAD, CONTRACT LINGUIST

So what's up today? There seems to be a problem at a local bank branch. The bank robbery squad, not the drug crimes squad, is responsible for investigating this case. So why were you called in?

Like all FBI agents, you have specialized skills and training that qualify you to be on teams that work with all of the squads in your field office. These team assignments are sometimes called "collateral jobs." So, in addition to being on the drug crimes squad,

The FBI is often called in to assist in major disaster situations like the collapse of this bridge in Minneapolis in 2007.

How flexible are you?

You're writing an essay for your history class, when your friend calls to say she's available to help you with the math that's been challenging you. You:

A Tell her that, even though you need the help, it's just not a good time to work on math. You know you'll never get your train of thought back if you leave the essay now.

B Are glad your friend finally found time to help you with math. It will be no problem to pick up on the essay again when you get back.

You had plans to go to the movies on Saturday night with your friends. Late in the afternoon, your neighbor calls. Her good friend is suddenly very ill and she really needs to go to the hospital to be with her. Can you please babysit her kids tonight? You:

A Tell her you can't possibly do that. She can't really expect you to change your plans at the last minute, can she?

B Get right over to her house to help her out. Emergencies are always more important than goofing off.

FBI agents have to be able to switch gears at a moment's notice. Crime doesn't happen on a schedule. Can you roll with the punches?

you are also part of the evidence response team. Other agents in your office have collateral jobs on the SWAT team, the special surveillance unit, or as computer experts, photographers, firearms specialists, trainers, and so on.

A Day as a Special Agent

The squad supervisor gives you a brief summary on the phone. The overnight cleaning crew came into the bank and was confronted by an incredible mess. It was clear that there had been a break-in. The cleaning crew knew that going in to start their jobs was probably not the smartest thing to do. After all, they didn't even know if the intruders were still in the bank.

The crew called their supervisor, who notified the bank manager. The bank manager notified the local police and they, of course, called the local FBI field office.

As soon as the operator at the field office got the call, she notified the supervisor of the squad assigned to bank robberies, who called his squad members to meet him at the bank. Knowing that the bank had been completely trashed, the squad supervisor also called in the field office's evidence response team—including you.

That may sound like a lot of calls, but FBI agents are used to moving quickly, and the whole process takes only a few minutes. And, speaking of moving quickly, that's exactly what you need to do right now. You throw on some clothes, grab your badge and gun (can't go anyplace without those two items), and head out to the scene.

Your first order of business is to talk to the squad supervisor or the lead agent on the case. She tells you that the local police have already determined that it is safe to go into the bank. She also lets you know that, at first glance, there doesn't seem to be any money missing and the safe appears to be secure. That may not be good news. Why did someone break into the bank? Was sensitive information taken? Were explosives planted? That remains to be seen. You get your specific assignment and head in to help process the site.

Your specialty is collecting "trace evidence," the material that a criminal leaves at a site and the material that the criminal takes from the site. Trace evidence can be critical in identifying a criminal and in proving the case against him at the trial.

You are extremely careful as you collect and package whatever you can find. You label everything clearly and in detail, sometimes asking the crime scene photographer to document where it was found. You treat every piece of evidence with great care; you never know what might be the very clue that breaks a case.

When you feel confident that every smidgen of evidence has been collected, you head back to your office. You will send some of the evidence to the crime lab in Washington; some will be analyzed right in your office. Other agents will search for more evidence in the bank's computer files, conduct interviews, and use all of the other FBI investigation techniques to solve the case.

Just Say No to Drugs

You get back to the office at 11:00 a.m., just in time for the update meeting of the Drug Task Force for your area. The Drug Task Force includes all of the agents on your squad plus employees of other law enforcement agencies who are permanently assigned to the FBI to work on this problem. Your task force includes police from other cities, towns, and counties in your state, the state police, the Drug Enforcement Agency, and the Secret Service.

It is critical that everyone involved in the anti-drug mission share everything they know. That way, each piece of data can be connected to form a big picture that can lead to major progress. For example, the police may have made arrests involving specific drugs that had not previously been seen in your area. Or a well-known location for drug dealing may have had no activity in recent days. Or a small-time robber picked up by the police lives

Agents go wherever they have to go to gather clues.

at the same address as someone suspected of importing drugs. All of that information can be helpful to your squad. Some of your information may be helpful to them as well.

FBI drug squads do not usually focus on small-time users of illicit drugs. That is the job of the local police. The FBI is concerned with stopping major drug trafficking and disrupting the organizations that manufacture, import, and distribute illicit drugs. One way they do this is to go after the leaders of the organizations and take the things that help the organizations stay in business: money, drugs, cars, and whatever else is valuable to them. The information that the members of the task force share helps each agency accomplish its part in solving the problem.

The meeting ends at 1:00 p.m. and you leave to grab a quick lunch. Just as you finish the last bite of your sandwich, your cell phone rings again. A building housing several families has been firebombed. One of the families that lived there was related to someone you've been investigating as part of a gang dealing in drugs. You know that this gang has been having disputes with a rival gang over who has the self-proclaimed right to sell on a certain corner. There may be a connection between the gang rivalry and the firebombing. You need to get to that crime scene as quickly as you can.

Before you leave, you take a moment to contact the victim assistance specialist. You know that the other families from the building will need immediate help. The FBI can help victims with emergency food, clothing, shelter, and interpretation services and the victim assistance specialist will get that ball rolling.

Putting the Pieces Together

Then it's off to the still smoldering building. You will protect the crime scene, collect evidence, and begin to interview witnesses. By 6:00 p.m., other agents have arrived to take over for you at the site. But, late as it is, you can't go home just yet.

Tomorrow morning you are scheduled to meet with an assistant U.S. attorney to review a case you recently handled. You're psyched for this meeting—totally determined to make sure everything is in perfect order so that the feds can go after a suspected drug dealer in court.

The suspect was found selling drugs in your area and is also implicated in a few home burglaries. Both of those crimes would usually be concerns for the local police, but this was not just a petty crime from a minor criminal.

Before he came to your area, your suspect had been arrested in another state. That arrest was for threatening an entire neighborhood so he could sell drugs on their streets. It was more than a little suspicious that shortly after the suspect's arrest, some important witnesses suddenly changed their minds about testifying against him. The suspect had been granted bail in that case and was free until his trial date.

The guy may be a vicious criminal, but he's not stupid. He knew that the trial would probably not have a happy ending for him. So what did he do? Skipped town and started over in a new area—yours!

Unfortunately for him, leaving a state to avoid prosecution put him right in the sights of the FBI, the people who are most likely to find him and bring him to trial on the new charges as well as the old ones. Which is exactly what you want to happen.

You have the authority to find the suspect, but you cannot make the decision to bring a case to trial. A prosecutor from the

FUN FACTOID

Every tiny bit of evidence can be important. The FBI lab needs only one forty-millionth of a drop of blood to identify a suspect.

Department of Justice or the U.S. Attorney's offices must present the case to a grand jury. Then it's up to the grand jury to bring the case to trial.

How can you help get this suspect to trial? First you had to carefully build your case. You collected physical evidence and background material. You sent some evidence to the lab at Quantico and requested specific tests that you thought would help the investigation. You interviewed suspects and witnesses, using your skills to encourage them to talk and to help them remember everything that happened. You researched everyone involved in the case (victims, suspects, and witnesses), looking for prior crimes and connections between any of those people. Now that you have put everything together in one big, well-organized file, you are ready to present it to an assistant U.S. attorney tomorrow.

It's been a long, hectic day. You worked hard, but you know you did your best to keep America safe—going after its criminals and protecting its people. When you finally leave the office, you know that you are one of the "good guys."

Help is On the Way

The FBI uses several specialized response teams.

Critical Incident Response Group. They rush in to help local field offices coordinate large scale operations like responding to the terrorist attacks on the World Trade Center in New York City and the aftermath of Hurricane Katrina in New Orleans.

Hostage Rescue Team. Hostage rescue team members are called in when people are being held against their will by by terrorists or criminals. They work alongside

Have I Seen You Somewhere Before?

You're at a restaurant with your family. Your mother seems to know the woman at the next table. You look over and:

A Have no idea who the woman is and pay no attention to your mother's conversation.

B Recognize the woman right away. Even though she is not wearing her usual doctor's coat and has her hair in a ponytail, you can still tell that it's the doctor you used to visit.

Special agents have to be able to remember a face they have seen in the files. They have to recognize that person wherever they see him or her, even if the person has different clothes, a different hairstyle or color, or is older than when the picture was taken.

specialists trained in negotiation, behavioral science, and communications to secure the release of the hostages. Armed force is always a last resort.

Behavioral Analysis Unit. Much like fictional "profilers," these agents use their experience and their knowledge of human behavior to help identify and capture some of the most unusual criminals, including serial killers.

SWAT Team. Each field office has its own SWAT (Special Weapons and Tactics) team made up of volunteers who have successfully completed the most rigorous training and are armed with high-powered weapons not usually used by other law enforcement and counterterrorist teams. They are called in when the FBI needs extra fire power to bring a situation under control.

Evidence Response Team. Some situations require very specialized skills to recover crime scene evidence. When evidence is underwater, for example, FBI divers are called in to swim through cold, dark water. They also use some amazing technology like miniature remote-controlled subs that send real-time color video to the surface for on-the-spot identification.

Disaster Squad. Natural disasters like hurricanes or tsunamis or non-natural disasters like airplane crashes often leave hundreds of victims. When that happens, specialists on this squad rush to the site to use their special skills to locate and aid survivors, as well as process fingerprints, palm prints, and footprints to help identify victims.

Shhh...It's a Secret

The U.S. Government has a uniform system for classifying, declassifying, and safeguarding national security information.

Confidential: Any materials or information that could be reasonably expected to cause *damage* to national security if disclosed.

Secret: Any materials or information that could be reasonably expected to cause *serious damage* to national security if disclosed.

Top Secret: Any materials or information that could be reasonably expected to cause *grave damage* to national security if they were disclosed.

CHAPTER 3

FBI Tech and Trends

Talk about having to change with the times! In the past decade, the FBI has experienced major changes in almost every area of the organization. Many of these changes have been made in response to the terrorist attacks on the United States on September 11, 2001. Other changes have been a result of advances in science that help agents solve crimes. And still more changes reflect the need to address new types of crimes that have come about as a result of new technology.

Preventing Attacks on the United States

In many ways, Americans are among the most fortunate people in the world. Think about this: almost every night the television news reports on someplace in the world where suicide bombers attacked large groups of citizens, missiles destroyed homes and businesses, or people are starving because war cut off the delivery of food and other necessities. In those countries, attacks are a horrible, but fairly common, part of everyday life.

Except for the attack on Pearl Harbor in 1941, Americans had not experienced a major attack on our soil until September 11, 2001, when terrorists killed almost 3,000

FUN FACTOID

Last year, the FBI received more than 12 million fingerprints that were submitted electronically. The bureau also got about 4.5 million that were sent the old-fashioned way, with inked cards.

"Time is not our friend in an emergency."

— PHIL EDNEY, FBI PUBLIC AFFAIRS SPECIALIST

people. Since then, the FBI has increased the emphasis on its mission to protect the United States from additional terror attacks. Here are just some of the things the FBI changed after 2001 to meet this new-challenge

- hired 2,000 additional employees

- more than doubled the number of intelligence analysts, to almost 2,200

- increased training for new FBI agents from 16 weeks to 18 weeks

- increased new agent training in counterterrorism, counterintelligence, and intelligence

- added 439 additional full-time linguists, with an emphasis on Arabic and Farsi (official languages of Iraq, Iran, and other countries)

- opened 13 new legal attaché offices in U.S. embassies and consulates around the world

Bringing the FBI into the Computer Age

Before 2001, very few FBI agents had access to the Internet. Since then, the FBI

FBI lab technicians become experts in analyzing very specific types of evidence such as explosives.

has added 30,000 computers, and now almost every agent can get online.

The fact that FBI agents could not access the Internet before 2001 isn't quite as bad as it might seem because in those days there wasn't much good information for the agents to find online. Since 9/11, the FBI has created a new database that now has more than 659 million records, including terrorist watch lists. About a quarter of that information comes from the FBI's records and criminal case files. The rest comes from other sources. For instance, the State Department provides input about passports that were reported lost or stolen, so agents can watch for people coming into our country under false identities. In addition, banks and other financial institutions provide information about suspicious cash deposits, so agents can be alert to groups that may be funding a terrorist organization or other types of criminal activity.

Remember that a lot of this information did exist in the past; it was just on different databases and not coordinated in any way. Imagine this situation: An agent on the East Coast is suspicious about the unusual travel of someone suspected of being part of al-Qaeda. At the same time, another agent, in another part of the country, is concerned that someone thought to be part of al-Qaeda is suddenly taking flying lessons. In fact, both agents could be looking at the same person. In the past, the two agents had no way to know that. Back then, the two pieces of information were just separate "dots," stored in different databases. It was not possible to "connect the dots" and identify that person as a threat.

Today, an FBI agent often has to check many names to narrow down the pool of suspects in an investigation. For example, if a department store was the target of bomb threats, the agent might first look at all current employees and employees who recently left their jobs there. The agent would want to know if any had a criminal history, if any were still in the area, if anyone who was recently fired had been in similar situations in the past.

Of course, even before the recent changes in technology, it would have been possible for an agent to check out 1,000 possible suspects. All the agent had to do was to run each name through 50 different databases—one-by-one. No sweat! It would only take a mere 32,222 hours. That's 1,343 days or more than

FIND OUT MORE

Fingerprints have many uses beyond solving crimes. Can you think of any? Check these FBI files to see some other ways fingerprint files have been useful: http://www.fbi.gov/page2/oct03/iafis100303.htm and http://www.fbi.gov/page2/dec05/border_iafis122705.htm.

three and a half years! As you've probably already concluded, this process was not particularly effective.

Today, an agent can check out 1,000 suspects in 30 minutes or less. Are law enforcement officers happy about that? You'd better believe it! In fact, more than 13,000 agents and analysts do an average of one million searches a month.

Technology has progressed even further than desktop computers. Many senior agents now carry wireless devices that combine a cell phone with the ability to send e-mail and surf the Internet. An agent on a stakeout can search for information about a suspect on the spot, and then send pictures and data to agents anywhere in the world.

New Crimes, New Clues

Most advances in technology bring wonderful things into our lives, but they can also introduce a lot of new problems. Take automobiles, for example. Cars make it easier to get places, stay in touch with friends and family, live farther away from our jobs, buy a lot of groceries at a time, and to have big, centrally located shopping centers. But cars bring bad news, too. "Getaway cars" make it easier for criminals to flee the scenes of their crimes. And the criminals can take more loot with them. Automobiles have also created the opportunity for new types of crime, such as drunk driving, carjackings, and auto theft.

Computer technology has worked in much the same way. While computers make it a lot easier to catch criminals, they also make life easier for criminals and have created whole new categories of crime.

FBI agents rely on computers to investigate or prevent terrorism. But there's another side to that story. For example, the terrorists who carried out the 9/11 attacks did much of their planning and communicating by e-mail. They did not have to meet

Cybercrime Wave

In August 2005, "Zotob," a malicious code, hit the Internet and caused countless computer systems around the world to sputter and crash. In the middle of CNN's news report on this, even the network's own computers went down. The  FBI immediately began to investigate. Using information from Microsoft and other private and public sector partners, they quickly determined that the worm probably began in Turkey or Morocco and sent out a Cyber Action Team. In less than eight days, the team found the people who had created this worm. Look for "Zotob" online and see what happened to these people.

in person, or worry about their phone lines being tapped, their mail being intercepted, or their meeting places being bugged. They used the Internet to send money to each other, check plane schedules, and find flight schools.

Now that computers are just about everywhere, they've made many new crimes possible: stealing secret information about the country's defense plans, distributing child pornography, sending viruses that shut down companies, hacking into computers to illegally change information or steal company secrets, stealing identities and credit card information, cyber-stalking, illegally downloading music, and making illegal copies of CDs and DVDs.

The FBI has developed new programs to fight these crimes. One of these programs created 93 computer crime task forces around the country. Computer Crime Task Forces (CCTFs) include members of the FBI, the Secret Service, the U.S. Postal Inspection Service, the Department of Defense, and the Internal

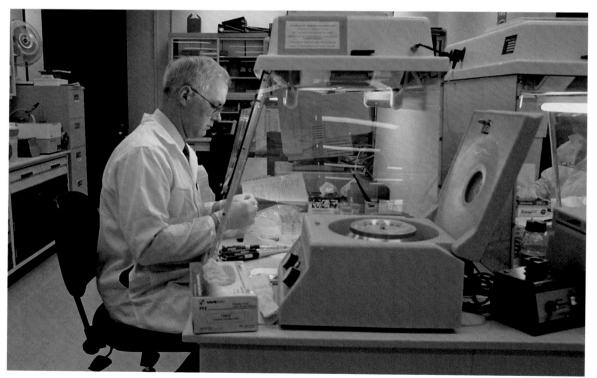

Teams of scientists at FBI labs use high-tech equipment to find evidence to crack cases.

Revenue Service, as well as the State Police, the State Attorney's Office, and local police departments. People from all of these agencies combine their specific knowledge, skills, resources, and investigative strategies into a unified attack on virtual crime.

A second program involves the Cyber Action Teams (CATs), which are small, highly trained teams of FBI agents, analysts, and computer experts. At a moment's notice, these teams can go any place in the world to respond to cyber intrusions. They also gather vital intelligence on emerging threats and trends that help identify the cybercrimes that are most dangerous to our national security and economy.

Identifying the "Perp"

When law enforcement agents try to identify a suspect in a crime, one of the first things they do is check for people who committed similar crimes in the past. The theory is that someone with a track record of a certain type of criminal act is more likely to strike again than it is for a typical law-abiding citizen to embark on a life of crime. The problem is confirming that past crimes were committed by the same person.

In 1882 Alphonse Bertillon, a clerk in a French police department, came up with a plan. He believed that if you could measure a lot of unchangeable things on a suspect or criminal after arresting him, you could create a profile specific to that person. Bertillon measurements included: body height, outstretched reach of both arms, trunk height, width of the head, length of the head, length of the right ear, width of the right ear, length of the left foot, length of the left middle finger, length of the left little finger, and length of the left forearm. This profile could then be used to determine if same person had been convicted of similar crimes in the past the next time he was arrested. It was a good idea, except that the person taking the measurements was not always precise, or the suspect was uncooperative, or as happened in one famous case, identical twins were involved. There had to be a better way!

A better way was found in the 1890s when an Argentine police officer, Juan Vucetich, began using fingerprint identification based on patterns identified by a British anthropologist, Sir Frances Galton. Fingerprints were found to be extremely reliable for

FUN FACTOID

The FBI currently has more than 250 million sets of fingerprint records on file. How many 8" by 8" cards does that represent? If you were to divide all the cards into 133 stacks, each one would be as high as the Empire State Building! In addition to that, the FBI gets more than a quarter of a million new ones every week (or about 37,000 every day).

identification. In fact, in the past 100 years, no two fingerprints have ever been found to be alike (even in identical twins).

The one drawback to this method was matching prints. It was easy for people to travel and to commit crimes in many different places. When investigators found fingerprints at a crime scene that they suspected might belong to someone who committed a similar crime in another place, they had to mail a sample of the prints to the other police department. That department then had to look through its fingerprint cards, and mail the matching prints back to the department that requested the information. The process took quite a lot of work and time.

The FBI's answer to that problem is the Integrated Automated Fingerprint Identification System (IAFIS), located in West Virginia. IAFIS was introduced in 1999. Today, the system has more than 49 million computerized fingerprint records for people with criminal records. Using this electronic system, law enforcement agencies can submit fingerprint search requests and receive a response within hours instead of the months it used to take.

Criminals don't always leave their prints at a crime scene, though. Many of them figure out ways to cover their tracks. In fact, less than 30 percent of weapons recovered from crime scenes have useful fingerprints on them. So what else can authorities use to identify people?

One answer is DNA, the genetic material that is different for every individual (except for identical twins). DNA is in every cell of your body, including your bones, hair, blood, and saliva. When the FBI first started testing DNA in 1989, the lab required a very large sample and the analysis took weeks. Today, all it takes is one cell, from a drinking glass, a postage stamp, a hair, or any other surface. Analysis is a lot faster now, too. Labs can get all the information they need in just a few days.

Like fingerprints, though, DNA from a crime scene is not very helpful unless there are samples to compare it to. Of course, the FBI is right on top of that, storing a database of DNA contributed from all 50 states.

CODIS, the FBI's Combined DNA Index System, actually has two different sets of records. One, the forensic index, contains DNA evidence found at crime scenes or from missing persons. The other, the offender index, contains the DNA profiles

CHECK IT OUT

The FBI has made it possible for you to follow a case from start to finish as it makes its way through various units of the FBI laboratory. Well, maybe it's not an actual case, but you can see what each unit of the lab does to process the evidence. FBI Investigates A Strange Flashlight: http://www.fbi .gov/kids/6th12th/ investigates/invest igates.htm.

of known offenders of sex offenses and other violent crimes. By using computers to exchange and compare DNA profiles, law enforcement agencies can link crimes to each other and to convicted offenders.

As of August 2006, CODIS had profiles for more than 3.5 million convicted offenders, and more than 148,000 forensic profiles of evidence found at crime scenes. The information stored in CODIS is so important that the server (main computer) that handles the information is hidden at a secret location.

Forensic Technology

The FBI lab has the equipment and experts to examine thousands of different kinds of evidence. Because most local law enforcement agencies cannot do that, the FBI sends experts to the scene when there is a major event like a terrorist bombing, a plane crash, or a train collision. Other times, the local agencies send their evidence to the FBI lab for examination and testing.

It's a bit mind-boggling to think about how highly specialized some of these FBI experts can be. For instance, some are especially knowledgeable about ballistics and might examine bullet holes in glass to determine the direction and sequencing of shots fired during the commission of a certain crime. Other experts might rely on an extensive background in chemistry to determine the exact type of abrasive material used to sabotage an industrial engine or machinery. Still other experts can use technology and their artistic skills to reconstuct what a crime victim's face looked like, using only skeletal remains. Even a tiny chip of paint can be enough evidence for experts to determine the exact make and model of a car involved in a series of bank robberies.

What's Next?

Biometrics, physical characteristic that distinguish one person from another, have long been used by law enforcement agencies. Fingerprints have been the most common biometric, with electronic scanning replacing the old inkpad method.

Other types of biometrics are coming into use, too, including facial recognition, hands, eye scans, or voices. Researchers are even looking at systems based on written signatures, personal

CHECK IT OUT

The Internet has made crime possible in many new ways. One way is fraud, cheating people out of their money. Check out the victim stories at http://www .LooksTooGoodToBe True.com/stories .aspx. Would you have fallen for any of these scams?

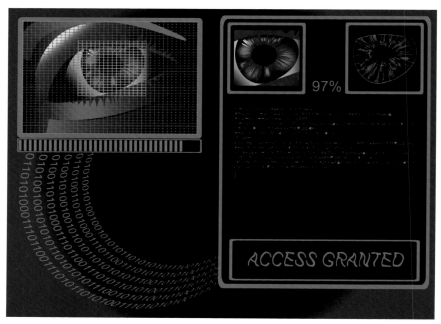

Biometric technology is a new, very precise tool used to identify people.

odors, ears, sweat pores, the way a person types on a keyboard, and body motions.

Some people predict that in 10 to 12 years some police officers will wear biometric scanners so they can determine the identities of suspects at the scene of their arrest. And if biometric scanners are integrated into ATM machines, check cashing facilities, or building entrance security systems, tracking suspects would become even easier.

Biometrics are already used for many things. In Iraq, some soldiers electronically fingerprint suspected insurgents, e-mail the fingerprints to a database, and see if there is already a record on that person. Some countries are experimenting with biometric passports. Schools are using biometric finger-scans to allow students to pay for lunch (and to allow parents to see what their children are buying). Some stores are using biometrics to make paying faster and to guard against identity theft.

The big news in crime-solving is brain fingerprinting. Brain fingerprinting can tell if someone recognizes something. It does not involve asking questions as traditional polygraph testing does, or "reading your mind." By connecting a type of headband to an EEG, a device that measures brain activity, a tester can see the specific brainwaves that occur when a suspect recognizes images, drawings, or words related to the crime.

Does brain fingerprinting work? In an experiment, FBI agents and civilians were tested with images and words that only FBI agents would know. The experiment identified every FBI agent, and did not falsely identify even one civilian! You can learn more about brain fingerprinting at http://www.pbs.org/wnet/innova tion/episode8.html.

Look for technology to improve airliner safety too. A group of companies in Europe is working on a system that could use sensors, cameras, microphones, and biometric devices to detect hijackers and automatically guide a plane to safety. The system could use biometrics to determine the identity of the pilot and flight crew and lock into a "safe mode" if anyone else tried to fly the plane. The safe mode would also have a system to navigate around tall buildings or mountain peaks.

This self-defending plane is scheduled to be operational between 2008 and 2010. It sounds like total fantasy now, but the idea of checking out 1,000 suspects in only 30 minutes seemed like an impossible dream just a few short years ago. Can you even imagine what new technologies you might be using as an FBI agent 20 years from now?

FUN FACTOID

One new FBI legal attaché is in Dubai, one of the United Arab Emirates. Cooperation from the Dubai police has already helped agents follow many counterterrorism leads, especially those that led to tracking terrorist money.

CHAPTER 4

FBI Agent in Training

FUN FACTOID

FBI firearms instruction starts with how to draw a gun while wearing a suit jacket. Each new agent fires 3,000 to 4,000 rounds of ammunition before graduating.

It's been a long morning. You finally have a minute to yourself. You settle into a booth at the local deli, order some breakfast, and suddenly hear shots ring out. You race to the window and see a sleazy-looking guy dash out of a beat-up car with gun drawn. At the same time, five young people come running from five different directions with their guns drawn. You hear the familiar, "Freeze. FBI!" More shots ring out. And before you know it, the sleazy guy is on the ground, hands cuffed behind him.

Whew! That's a little too much excitement before breakfast. It's even worse coming on the heels of yesterday's lunch that was interrupted by a hold-up at the savings and loan bank just down the street.

You're thinking that this is a little too weird, that maybe you should be a little more careful about planning your travel. And then you remember. You're in Hogan's Alley, "the baddest town in America."

Hogan's Alley is a realistic training facility that is just one aspect of the 18-week training for new FBI agents. But first, you have to qualify to be in the training. Think you could make it? Let's find out.

> "We don't want **real felons on the job.** This is not a **training** ground for **bank robbers** or dope dealers."

— JIM PLEDGER, A FORMER INSTRUCTOR AT THE FBI ACADEMY

First Steps

Not just anyone can become an FBI agent. To qualify for consideration as an FBI agent, you must be a U.S. citizen, between 23 and 36 years old. You need a four-year degree from an accredited college or university, at least three years of professional work experience, and a valid driver's license. You also have to qualify for one of the following special agent entry programs:

FBI agents have to be prepared to defend themselves and protect others from dangerous criminals.

• **Accounting.** To qualify for the accounting entry program, you must be certified as a CPA (Certified Public Accountant) or have a four-year business degree with additional credits in accounting and business law and two years' of relevant work experience.

• **Computer Science/Information Technology.** The computer science/information technology entry program requires that you have a degree in computer or information technology, a degree in electrical engineering, or a B.A. (bachelor of arts) or B.S. (bachelor of sciences) plus other computer certification.

Agent-in-Training

When you think about going to college and then working in your chosen field for two years before you apply to the FBI, you:

A Try to find a way to get around the requirement.

B Figure you can put up with it, if it paves the way for becoming an FBI agent.

C Think it will be a great opportunity to learn a lot so you can make a contribution right away.

(Hint: If you picked one of the first two choices, you may want to think about why you really want to be an FBI agent.)

You are bowling with a close friend. You:

A Don't pay much attention to how well either of you score. It's just nice to be with your friend.

B Think this is a good opportunity to try some new techniques. You may have a low score today, but you will be much better next time.

C Are determined to win. All the time.

(Hint: Good FBI agents know that they always need to improve their skills.)

You finished all your homework and all your house chores. You are just about to sit down to watch your favorite TV show, when your grandparents show up, and your parents ask you to spend some time with the family. You

A Try to convince your parents to let you watch your show. You've been waiting for it all week, and it's not fair for you to miss it.

B Go with the flow. It will be good to make your grandparents happy, and there can't be that much happening on this week's episode of the show.

(Hint: Some words for FBI agents to live by might be, "Expect the unexpected." You will always have to be ready for a change in plans.)

• **Language.** If you're interested in the language entry program, you need to have a B.S. or B.A. degree in any discipline and proficiency in a language that meets the needs of the FBI. The FBI won't just take your word for your language ability. You will have to prove it with tests of listening, reading, and speaking.

• **Law.** The law entry program requires a J.D. (juris doctorate) degree from an accredited law school.

• **Diversified.** If you don't have one of the above specialized backgrounds, you can still qualify under the diversified entry program, a type of "everything else" category. You must have a B.S. or B.A. degree in any discipline, plus three years of full-time work experience, or an advanced degree accompanied by two years of full-time work experience.

Okay, you qualify for one of the five programs, and you're ready to sign up. Not so fast. First you have to show that you have one or more of the critical skills the FBI is looking for.

These include critical skills that can be demonstrated by experience like

• **Intelligence Experience.** You have already worked for two years in an intelligence area in the FBI or elsewhere, or you have a degree in international studies, international finance, or a closely related discipline.

• **Law Enforcement Experience.** You have at least two years of full-time investigative experience in a law enforcement agency.

• **Military Experience.** You have two years of substantial, full-time work experience in the military.

• **Physical Sciences Expertise.** You have a degree in a scientific field such as biology, biochemistry, chemistry, forensics, mathematics, medical specialties, nursing, or physics.

Now that you qualify to apply to be an FBI agent, you can move on to the two written tests and an interview. Get through those and you're eligible for a qualifying physical fitness test (push-ups, anyone?). After that you'll have to pass a background

FUN FACTOID

It's not enough just to survive being pepper sprayed. To pass this assignment, you will also have to open at least one eye, protect your gun from a trainee trying to grab it, force that trainee down onto the ground, and then yell, "FBI! Don't move!"

check that qualifies you for top-secret security clearance. The background investigation includes everything from a polygraph examination to interviews with past employers and neighbors to verification of your educational achievements. Your background needs to be really, really clean, meaning you have never been arrested, you have no history of major drug use, and you have never been fired under bad circumstances.

And one last detail… you have to be completely available for assignment anywhere in the FBI's jurisdiction.

No sweat, right? Wrong! For every 10,000 people who apply to the FBI only about 150 are accepted for training.

Suppose you're one of the lucky ones to make the cut. Congratulations! It's time to head out to the FBI Training Academy in Quantico, Virginia, where you will live on campus with the other trainees.

Did you stay in shape while you were waiting to be cleared for the academy? Good thing! You have to re-take the physical fitness test during your first week there (and again later on).

The Academy

Your academy training will include classroom lessons in law, behavioral science, interviewing techniques, ethics, and forensic science. Yes, you will have to pass tests on all of those classes! You will have a lot of practical lessons too.

Think you can defend yourself? This is the place to learn. No one wants you to get hurt during training, so you'll wear boxing gloves, headgear, and mouth guards. Then, in the safety of the academy gym, you'll practice defending yourself against a group of attackers. What about pepper spray? Chance of a lifetime! You'll get to experience what it's like to be sprayed for two reasons: first, to know you can survive it; second, to know what it feels like before you use it on someone else.

What about those interrogations you see on the crime shows? Sure, the TV cops make it look easy, but there are real skills involved. The academy will teach you how to interview a suspect and then move in for a confession.

Competency with firearms is one of the most basic and important skills for a new agent. During your training you will become familiar and confident with the handguns, shotguns, and other

FIND OUT MORE

FBI field offices sponsor guest speakers who can come to your school, junior special agent programs, and citizen academies. All programs have to be requested by an adult who is part of an official organization, and only adults over 21 can participate in the citizen academies. Are you really excited to learn more about the FBI? See if your school or community group would like to participate. Check out the possibilities at http://www.fbi.gov/hq/ood/opca/outreach/copintro.htm.

weapons that are issued. You will become extremely familiar and confident with the firearm that is personally issued to you, as you take full responsibility for its cleaning and maintenance. In your career as an agent, the one thing you must be able to totally rely on is the proper functioning of your weapon. You cannot depend on anyone else to maintain it for you.

Your agent training will also include driving lessons. Think you will know how to drive by the time you are ready for the FBI Academy? Maybe you will be able to handle "civilian" driving by then, but this course will teach you the defensive and offensive driving tactics that may help you make an arrest or save your life.

About eight weeks into the training, you're ready for the big time.

Hogan's Alley

Hogan's Alley is a pretend town at the FBI Academy. It has everything a regular town would have: stores, restaurants, a bank, a movie theater, a motel, and lots of people and traffic. What makes this town special is that there are major crimes several times a day, every day of the year. And every criminal is apprehended.

The "town" is populated with actors who play the roles of criminals and bystanders, and the actors are encouraged to make nothing easy for you. Your first experience in Hogan's Alley may be a lesson in surveillance. You may have to track a suspect and observe him in an illegal act. That may be followed by an arrest of an unarmed suspect. All of the instructors at the academy are former agents. They watch your every move, teaching you the best way to frisk a suspect, read him his rights, put on handcuffs, and fill out an arrest form. Every detail counts, even how forcefully you yell, "Freeze! FBI!"

You advance to subduing resistant suspects, facing armed felons, and even testifying in a pretend court where your hard work

Good Stuff

In order to graduate from the FBI Academy, you must do more than successfully complete the training program. You also have to show that you follow the FBI Core Values:

A Rigorous obedience to the constitution of the United States

B Respect for the dignity of all those we protect

C Compassion

D Fairness

E Uncompromising personal integrity and institutional integrity

How can you begin to develop those values in your current life?

FIND OUT MORE

to gather evidence on a case may be thrown out if it was not properly obtained. The training is intense and there are always surprises. What do you do if the loudspeakers on your police car malfunction during a hostage crisis? What if a "suspect" pulls a plastic gun on you because you didn't search him well enough? Hogan's Alley is not easy. But it's a lot better to make mistakes there than in the real world.

In week 17, you will take your final firearms tests. First, the targets. No problem. All you have to do is hit a target 120 times out of 150 shots from four different positions and four different distances. Then the really tough one—the firearms training simulation (FATS). You've used FATS throughout your training. It can be a scary experience.

You sit in a dark room, watching a large screen. The video you watch is a realistic reenactment of an event involving FBI

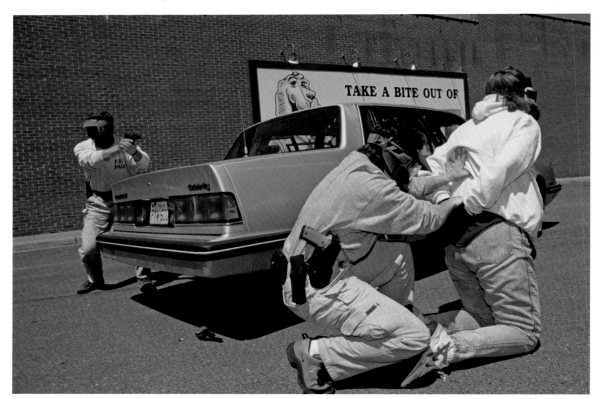

Hogan's Alley is where FBI agent trainees practice responding to dangerous situations.

agents and an armed criminal. You need to bring down the criminal and save the other agents. You, and you alone, must make all the decisions. Do you shoot? If so, when? Shoot too quickly and you might hurt an innocent person. Shoot too late, and you might be the one on the ground. Just like in life, the crisis moment is so fast that you're not quite sure what you just did or what the outcome was.

Fortunately, the training exercise has slow motion replay. You did it! You got the bad guy—without shooting the other agents by mistake.

Welcome to the FBI

Congratulations! You're a special agent. You survived the training, passed all the tests, and have been issued your official special agent badge.

As a new special agent, you will be assigned to one of the FBI's 56 field offices, probably a small or medium-sized one. Of course, your assignment is based on the FBI's needs, not your preferences. You will probably remain in your first assignment for about three years, unless the program needs you someplace else. For your first two years, you will be on probation, and guided by a veteran special agent who will help you apply your academy training to real life.

Getting Started Now

It's not too early to start thinking about a career with the FBI. You'll have to go to college and earn excellent grades, so you might want to start developing some good study habits now. You'll have to be in really good physical shape too, so get used to working out and training. Oh, and one more thing. You'll have to stay out of trouble. Get a criminal record and say good-bye to any hope you have of becoming an FBI agent.

The FBI looks for people who are motivated and who have strong leadership qualities. Look for opportunities to see if you like being a leader. Join a team, a club, or a community group, and see where you can make a contribution.

Being an FBI agent is a great career. It takes hard work to become one, and hard work to be a good one. But the people who do it think it's the best job in the world!

All FBI employees from special agents to receptionists must qualify for top-security clearance before they can begin working. Once hired, they must maintain their eligibility for a top-secret security clearance, undergo a limited background check every five years, and submit to random drug tests throughout their careers.

CHAPTER 5

The FBI Team

Does the idea of being part of the FBI's fight against crime and terrorism appeal to you? There are hundreds of ways to participate. Only 40 percent of FBI employees are special agents. The rest are professional support personnel, who are just as important as special agents. The difference is that support personnel do not carry guns or badges, do not have the authority to make an arrest, and do not go through the same training at the FBI Academy. The jobs in this chapter are usually performed by support personnel. Some special agents may also be qualified to do them.

Artists and Graphic Designers

Sometimes a good artist can help solve a crime. A composite drawing, created from the memory of a witness, can help the FBI identify a suspect or rule out potential suspects. Artists can help give agents an idea of how someone might look after a lot of time has passed.

Community Outreach Specialist

The FBI needs people with backgrounds in sociology or similar fields. As Tammy Peter, a community outreach specialist

FUN FACTOID

It's not a forever thing. You can only work as a special agent until you reach the age of 55. After that, it's retirement from the FBI or moving on to a professional support position.

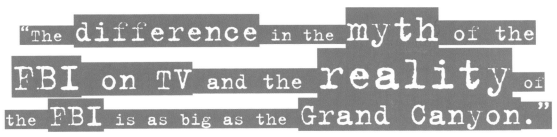

"The difference in the myth of the FBI on TV and the reality of the FBI is as big as the Grand Canyon."

RON WOODS, HUMAN PERFORMANCE INSTITUTE

says, "… our job is mainly to build bridges where there are none, so that people will be open and receptive to the FBI and willing to help and support us." Community outreach professionals help crime witnesses and victims work with schools and businesses and create local programs such as citizens' FBI academies and adopt-a-school.

Chemist

FBI chemists are critical to many investigations. They analyze and measure drugs, explosives, and other suspect substances. Some chemists can identify the make, model, and year of a car with just a small chip of paint. They check suspects, victims, crime scenes, and food products for the presence of drugs or poisons. They also help track suspects in bank robberies when banks include "dye packs" (hidden devices that burst and release a colorful, staining substance) in the stolen money.

Cryptographer

One critical job of the FBI is to "break" ciphers or codes to find out what criminals or enemies are saying to each other. Another important job is to put plans and information from the FBI or other government agencies into codes that others cannot break. Cryptographers are the specialists who do this. Cryptographers use both ciphers and codes, two methods that accomplish the same thing in different ways. Ciphers use a letter or symbol in the message to represent another letter, like in Morse code. Codes use words or phrases to stand for other words, like "bling" for "jewelry," or LOL or BRB ("laugh out loud" or "be right back" in cyber chat).

NAME: Patricia O'Hare Boudreau

OFFICIAL TITLE: Intelligence Analyst

What do you do?

As an intelligence analyst, I provide analytical and operational support to international and domestic terrorism investigations. I work directly with FBI special agents to identify important information about the subjects of our investigation. I use classified and unclassified computer databases to find information. I write intelligence reports for FBI special agents and other law enforcement agencies that may benefit from my information.

I work in a team environment of analysts who have different backgrounds, including counterintelligence, cybercrime, and criminal investigations. We combine or "pool" our resources to help each other meet our deadlines. Our teamwork helps keep America a safe place to live. I am very proud to work for the FBI.

How did you get started?

My parents felt strongly about the United States, and always reminded my four siblings and me how lucky we were to be growing up in this country. They were strong role models and active in the schools and politics of our community. They made me realize the importance of serving my community and my government.

In college, I majored in political science and minored in business. As a senior, I was chosen for a very competitive internship position at my state capital. I was soon hired as a legislative research consultant, getting a salary and 15 college credits. After college, that job was eliminated. I looked in the phone book and wrote to every government agency that might want a college graduate with my background. I was surprised to hear from the New Haven FBI office. I was interviewed and tested. They investigated my background, and I was hired in 1985 for a support position. This was unusual because most college graduates were coming into the FBI as special agents.

One year later, I was promoted to technical information specialist. That job was exciting and challenging, and I got to travel throughout the United States. During the past 20 years, I have been to training sessions at the FBI Academy at Quantico and to FBI headquarters. I have also assisted on high profile investigations at many different field offices.

FBI Police Officer

The FBI has its own police force to protect FBI employees, buildings, and the streets around those buildings. Their most important task is to prevent or respond to terrorist attacks and other criminal acts. FBI police are stationed at the FBI headquarters and field office in Washington, D.C., at the FBI Academy and laboratory at Quantico, at the New York City field office, and at the Criminal Justice Information Services Division in Clarksburg, West Virginia.

Fingerprint Examiner

Fingerprint examiners do more than match fingerprints to help current investigations. Some of them are also on the disaster squad, where they use their skills to identify crime victims. FBI examiners may be called on to check fingerprints to make sure these contractors have no criminal record.

Financial Analyst

The saying "show me the money" also describes a useful crime-fighting tool. FBI financial analysts say that going through financial records gets their hearts racing. By following the flow of money all over the world, they have prevented planned terrorist acts, put major drug lords out of business, and stopped some of the cheating on health care insurance that costs the United States more than $100 billion a year.

Forensic Scientist

Forensic scientists analyze everything that comes into the lab, from tire tread marks to DNA. They investigate bomb fragments, bullets, forgeries, hazardous materials, poisons, and trace evidence. If you need information on anything, there's probably an expert at the FBI lab who can provide it.

Information Technology Specialist

Information technology (IT) professionals, or computer specialists, work at headquarters and at field offices to develop and maintain all of the FBI computers and programs, just like the help desk at a school or business. But these professionals provide much more than just technical support. IT professionals identify cybercrimes and prevent new ones. They support FBI investigations and provide state-of-the- art identification and information services to local, state, federal, and international criminal justice partners.

Intelligence Analyst

Intelligence analysts get and analyze information about an enemy or a potential enemy. Of course, the information an intelligence analyst needs is not exactly out in the open, waiting to be found. In fact, it is almost always secret or very hard to find. Intelligence analysts get information from many different sources, including foreign powers, criminal groups, and terrorist organizations. It takes a lot of digging, and the analysts have to know a lot about each of the groups they are looking at, including the group's leaders and members, what the group has done in the past, its goals, and its current members and their connections. While many intelligence analysts gather information, others combine the results, looking for common connections or contradictions. If they think all this information relates to a current FBI operation, they make sure it gets out to every FBI employee who is working on a relevant project.

Investigative Specialist

Investigative specialists work behind the scenes to analyze information and look for patterns, putting the clues and evidence together to make strong cases. They also plan all aspects of surveillance operations.

Language Specialist

The FBI needs trustworthy people to accurately translate and analyze communications like videotapes from a terrorist group, demands from a hostage-taker, or local newspaper reports. They also need people who can translate between English and another language so agents can communicate with sources who do not speak English. FBI language specialists are part translators and part investigators. They may have to interview victims, witnesses, or suspects, or identify coded communications and messages. They often add comments based on their knowledge of cultural meanings of some of the messages.

NAME: **Phil Edney**
OFFICIAL TITLE: **Public Affairs Specialist**

What do you do?

There are two sides to this unit: investigative publicity and public affairs. I work on the public affairs side. The investigative publicity side of my unit is responsible for publicizing the open and unsolved cases that are listed on the FBI top ten lists.

As a public affairs specialist, I help people who want to learn more about the FBI. I talk to reporters for newspapers and magazines, people who are writing books about the FBI (like this one), and people who want to have authentic background information for fiction books.

Another part of my job is to work with film and television productions. I answer questions from the writers and review scripts for accuracy. When I am assigned to a production that has permission to film at FBI headquarters, I coordinate their interviews with the department they want to incorporate into their project. I arrange for the actual location filming, and provide any other assistance that is needed.

I have been involved with some feature films and with many TV shows, such as *Criminal Minds, Numbers, America's Most Wanted*, and *FBI Files*. I've also worked with The Discovery Channel, A&E, National Geographic (magazine and television), Japanese television, and British television.

How did you get started?

I was in the Army for 20 years and served in the military police. When I left the military, I worked for a private company in Georgia that provided security for the State Department. That led to a job with the FBI police.

Working for the FBI fit right in with my past experience. In the military, I had been a military police investigator (a job comparable to being a city detective) and a military criminal investigator (a lot like an FBI investigator).

Eventually I decided that I wanted something a little less risky than police work. I heard about an opening in the public affairs office, and went for it.

I love this work. I get to learn about every department in the FBI and I get to talk to very interesting authors, reporters, and production people.

NAME: Annie Pardo

OFFICIAL TITLE: Visual Information Specialist, Counterintelligence Division

What do you do?

I am a designer and I prepare printed materials, Web site materials, exhibits, and videos for the National Security Branch (NSB). I also do some research and editing. I recently created a brochure and video about what the NSB does. These materials will be sent to law enforcement agencies all over the country to encourage them to share information and work more closely with us.

ON THE JOB

For example, a local police department contacted us when they found a car that was broken into and the stolen items included important military plans. When the FBI and the local police worked together, they were able to find the person who had taken this important information.

How did you get started?

In college, I majored in studio art and I have a graduate degree in museum exhibition design. While I was in graduate school, I worked for the Smithsonian Museum doing some design work and coordinating special events. When I finished school, I worked as a senior designer in a company that did work for the Department of Justice. That company was having some financial problems, so when I heard about an opening at the FBI, I went for it and got the job.

Photographer

FBI photographers document evidence, crime scenes, subjects, and victims. The work requires more than knowledge of photography. FBI photographers may work in extreme weather conditions, from very high places, or from small planes or helicopters. They must remain calm and professional at the scene of a violent crime or a natural disaster.

Public Affairs Specialist

The public affairs office is responsible for getting the word about the FBI out to the public, as well as for consulting on television shows and movies about the FBI. The public affairs office uses press releases to tell newspapers, television, and radio about news from the FBI, keeps the FBI Web site updated, and supports community relations programs. You can read transcripts of the FBI's weekly radio show at http://www.fbi.gov/thisweek/ar chive/radarchive.htm or learn about the FBI's Closed Case of the Week at http://www.fbi.gov/gotcha/archive/gotarchive.htm.

Surveillance Specialist

Surveillance specialists are assigned to FBI field offices. Their purpose is to learn everything they can about a person or group that is potentially dangerous. In order to do this, surveillance specialists use many high-tech gadgets, such as listening devices and hidden cameras. The subjects of their surveillance may be suspected terrorists groups, suspected spies within our own country, or suspected criminals. Any field agent may do surveillance as part of an investigation, but these specialists have the latest training and up-to-the-minute equipment.

Victim Assistance Specialist

Victims of federal crimes investigated by the FBI are eligible for help in getting their lives back together. Victim assistance specialists can help access victim compensation funds and get emergency assistance funds. They can accompany victims to medical services or to court, and direct them to appropriate counseling services. Crime victims also have the right to be notified about court proceedings and the custody status of the offender. Victim assistance specialists make sure that happens. In addition to victim assistance specialists across the United States, the FBI also has a special terrorism victim assistance team that works out of FBI headquarters.

CHAPTER 6

Kids Ask, FBI Agents Answer

Still have questions about what the FBI is all about? So did a group of curious middle schoolers from Fairfield County, Connecticut. We asked Alec W., Caroline B., Emily F., Gabrielle F., Greg Z., and Noah B. to share what they wanted to know and then went straight to the source—FBI special agents—to find answers.

As you know by now, FBI agents do really important work to keep our country safe. They are not allowed to talk about many of the things they do. In fact, some agents cannot even reveal their names or what they look like. Fortunately, three *very* special agents were able to take time from their incredibly busy schedules to share some of their inside info with us.

Special Agent Jeffrey Berkin has been with the FBI for 23 years. Today he is Deputy Assistant Director for Security for the entire FBI. Special Agent William Reiner, with the FBI for 21 years, is now a squad supervisor in an FBI field office. Special Agent Katherine W. Schweit, an FBI agent for 10 years, is a supervisory agent at FBI headquarters, currently coordinating all training for the National Security Branch.

What do you do and what is it like?

– Gabrielle F.

Special Agent Berkin: I am a deputy assistant director of the FBI, assigned to the security division at FBI headquarters. The security division protects the people, information, operations, and facilities of the FBI. Being in charge of this division means that I have to make sure that all 30,000 employees at all of our 700 locations around the world are safe.

Special Agent Reiner: I am a supervisory special agent for Squad 4 in the New Haven field office. Squad 4 is responsible for organized crime, violent gangs, drug investigations, and investigations of crimes like kidnappings and bank robberies. I supervise 25 agents and two task forces.

Gabrielle F.

Special Agent Schweit: Right now I work in Washington, D.C., at FBI headquarters. I started as a field agent, working bank robberies and recruiting people who would be able to give me information if I had to investigate domestic and international terrorism cases in the future. After seven years, I was promoted to a supervisor position and taught in the counterintelligence training center. When the National Security Branch was created in 2005, I was assigned to coordinate all training for the 15,000 members of the branch. There are more than one hundred joint terrorism task forces, and everyone has to have the same understanding of the mission.

Jeffrey Berkin

What makes being an FBI agent fun and more than just a job?

— Greg Z.

Special Agent Reiner: Working for the FBI is not a job; it is a total way of life. You never know what is going to happen next. For me, one of the cool things is that I get to know about everything that happens in the state before everyone else. Later, when it is on the news, I not only know about it, but I have also been involved in it.

Special Agent Berkin: My job is great. It is always very busy, with many different challenges to be addressed every day.

Special Agent Schweit: I love being a special agent. It's great to be one of the "good guys."

Did you grow up knowing you would be an FBI Agent? What did you think you would be?

— Alec W.

Special Agent Berkin: I always wanted to be an FBI agent.

Special Agent Schweit: Since I was very young, I wanted to be a journalist. I worked for the school newspaper in high school, a real daily newspaper when I was in college, and a newspaper in Chicago after graduation. I'm always looking for a new challenge, so I went to law school at night, and finally left the newspaper to practice law as a state prosecutor (the lawyer who tries to prove the defendant is guilty). My cousin, an agent himself, told me about the special agent job. It seemed like it would be another exciting challenge, and I went for it.

Special Agent Reiner: My plan was to play for the New York Yankees. I did play baseball in high school and college, but I soon realized that I wasn't going to be a Yankee. When I was a senior in college, I spoke to an FBI recruiter. The job sounded exciting and different, something in which I would not be sitting at a desk every day. My college major was in accounting, a skill the FBI was strongly interested in.

What types of training did you have to undergo to become an agent?

— Noah B.

Special Agent Berkin: I applied to be a special agent while I was in my last year of law school. I had to take a written test, interview with three special agents, and have a medical examination and a background investigation. It took about two years from the time I applied until I was offered a job.

Special Agent Reiner: I joined the FBI when I was 23, which was the youngest age allowed. Although I did not have three years of practical experience, my college major was accounting, one of the skills the FBI was looking for.

Special Agent Schweit: My cousin convinced me to apply to the FBI just before Christmas, and by June 1 had been invited to the FBI Training Academy in Quantico. I was as surprised as anyone to get feedback so quickly. I had to pass two tests, a medical exam, a polygraph exam, an interview, and a background check before I was eligible for 16 weeks of training at the academy. I knew the academy would be tough so, before I even got there, I started running and doing pushups and sit-ups to help me through the program.

Noah B.

How hard was training? — Alec W.

Special Agent Berkin: I am an attorney, so the legal and other academic instruction was not difficult for me. On the other hand, I had never participated in a regular exercise program before joining the FBI, so I found the physical fitness activities and standards to be quite difficult. I thought firearm training was easy and fun.

The academy was tremendously exciting. We were getting paid to exercise regularly, to shoot, and to learn how to investigate serious crimes. We were going to be FBI special agents—what could be more exciting than that?

Special Agent Reiner: Training was definitely exciting. Some people used to call it "college with guns." I was in the first class at the FBI to use Hogan's Alley as part of the course. We knew that we were in training and that everyone else was acting, but it was amazing how real everything seemed.

Special Agent Schweit: When I started the training program at the FBI Academy I was 36, much older than most new agents. The FBI expects special agents to be tough, and the physical training is hard for everyone. The training I did before

Katherine Schweit

I began the program didn't help enough. There were eight women in my class in addition to myself. After four months of training, we had each lost at least one dress size.

What were some of your missions?

– Caroline B., Emily F.

Special Agent Berkin: My first assignments included handling bank robberies and kidnappings, and serving as a sniper on the Minneapolis FBI SWAT Team. I interviewed victims of violent crimes, witnesses, and suspects, and prepared my cases for prosecution by the United States Attorney's Office whenever appropriate. I also participated in surveillance activities and in arrests. As part of the SWAT team, I participated in missions involving the execution of search and arrest warrants in cases involving domestic terrorists and drug dealers.

Later in my career, I was assigned to classified counterintelligence matters. I identified hostile intelligence services directed against the United States and then disrupted those efforts.

Special Agent Reiner: My squad is responsible for organized crime, violent gangs, drug investigations, and reactive investigations for crimes like kidnappings and bank robberies.

Special Agent Schweit: Part of the job of FBI special agents who work National Security is to hunt down spies and terrorists in the United States. Although I've followed, photographed, and helped report many such individuals, national security work is classified and I can't discuss the details.

Caroline B.

What is the most important assignment you ever did?

– Gabrielle F.

Special Agent Berkin: Every assignment was very important in its own way. Some of the counterintelligence cases I worked on resulted in the prosecution and conviction of spies who attempted to cause grave harm to our national security. I consider those to be particularly important successes.

Special Agent Reiner: Every assignment is very important to the people involved. I am especially proud of the cases where I could see the direct impact on someone. I've had four kidnapping cases and we rescued the person all four times. It is just incredible to return a kidnapped child to a parent or to know that you have saved a life.

Special Agent Schweit: It's hard to choose but I can think of two important assignments. The first was on September 11, 2001, when I began supervising my field office's portion of the terrorism investigation. Nothing is more important than

Emily F.

the safety of the people in the United States; that's my most important job. No one in the FBI was the same after that day because we had tried so hard before then and still couldn't prevent the attack.

The second case was the most important to the victim. A woman who was 88 years old and 88 pounds was kidnapped for ransom on a cold March morning and held for five days in a snowmobile trailer outside the kidnapper's home. The kidnapper thought he would get a million dollars from the woman's family, but instead he went to jail for a long time. We used real time tracking of the kidnapper's computer transmissions from cyber cafes and his cell phone transmissions to find him, and our skilled hostage negotiator talked him into telling us where the victim was held.

I was on the radio in the command post when the SWAT team arrived at the trailer and radioed in that she was found alive. "What took you so long?" she asked them. She was one tough lady and that was definitely my proudest day as a special agent.

What cool gadgets do you use?

– Emily F., Greg Z.

Special Agent Schweit: Because I work in National Security, I have worked with lots of really cool gadgets but the existence of most of them is classified as secret and so I can't share. Sorry! Some of the nonclassified items I have worked with include binoculars and digital and video equipment that can see in the pitch-black darkness and others that are so powerful that I can hide a block away from my target. Of course, I have pepper spray and handcuffs, which are very handy gadgets for arrests.

Special Agent Berkin: I have used night vision goggles to allow me to see in the dark, and special telephones and radios that permit top secret conversations without a risk that the wrong people might overhear me. When I was on the

Minneapolis SWAT team, I had a sniper rifle equipped with a bipod and telescope; working with the Milwaukee SWAT team, I had a fully automatic assault rifle equipped with a laser aiming device. In Los Angeles, I was assigned the use of a Porsche 911 Cabriolet for operational purposes. I've used a lot of interesting technologies in investigations to stop spies, but I can't tell you about them.

How many criminals have you caught? Can you tell me about an interesting criminal you captured?

– Caroline B.

Special Agent Berkin: I don't know how many arrests I have participated in, because I have not kept count. I'm unable to discuss particular cases.

Special Agent Reiner: Hundreds and hundreds and hundreds. I haven't kept count.

Special Agent Schweit: I have never kept track of how many criminals I've caught because special agents are involved in many, many arrests in their careers. One criminal I was especially happy to help send to jail was a guy who was teaching teenagers to shoot automatic weapons so they could join in a race war that he and others wanted to start. When we arrested him, we had to devise a special plan, because he lived with his 80-year-old grandmother and we didn't want her to get hurt. We tricked him into coming out of the house at 6:00 a.m. and when he was safely away from the door, we got him.

Our SWAT team found a loaded AK-47 style automatic assault rifle hidden in a compartment by the door he had just exited. He had more than a dozen loaded guns hidden in different places in the house and buried around the outside of his home.

CHAPTER 7

Virtual Apprentice
FBI AGENT FOR A DAY

Ready to take the virtual apprentice challenge and find out what it's like to be an FBI agent for a day? You'll need paper and pencils, Scotch tape, ruler, and yardstick. If you have them in the house, it would be helpful to have: a digital camera, plastic zip bags, and a magnifying glass.

9:00 FBI agents have to stay in shape and be ready for whatever comes up each day. Go for a run around your neighborhood, or do some indoor calisthenics. Then have a healthy breakfast to fuel up for the day. (Hint: Donuts and cola are not going to sustain your energy level for the day.)

10:00 Try a "blood" spatter experiment. You'll need a small cup of water that has been tinted with red food coloring, a clean medicine dropper, a few sheets of plain paper, a ruler, and a yardstick. Cover the floor with newspaper to protect it, then place a sheet of plain paper on top of it. Hold the dropper about six inches above the paper and drip one drop of liquid onto the sheet. Write down the height you dropped the "blood" from and the diameter of the spatter. Repeat the process, increasing the distance each time (use your yardstick to measure the height). Use a new sheet of paper each time, and be sure to record the height and diameter each time. How can this kind of experiment help investigators at the scene of a crime?

11:00 You and your partner often need to get messages to each other —messages that no one else must be able to read. Devise some different codes that you can use for your messages. For ideas, check out http://www.nsa.gov/kids or http://www.nationalgeographic.com/ngkids/trythis/secretcodes. Today's message is: "Meet me at noon. I will carry a blue book."

12:00 Lunch! Try to stay on the high-protein, high-energy side.

1:00 Practice your witness interviewing skills. Find a picture in a newspaper or magazine that has several people in it. Make a list of questions that you might ask people who "witnessed" the scene in the picture. Your questions might be about what was happening in the picture, descriptions of the people, or other details in the scene. Round up friends or family to play the role of "witnesses" for your practice. Let each "witness" view the scene for 30 seconds before your interview. Write down the answers you get. Did your "witnesses" all give the same answers? Were they correct?

2:00 Check your own powers of observation and recall. Take a quick walk to the end of your street or through some rooms of your house. Return to your desk and list as many details as you can about what you saw on your walk. Redo your walk. How many details did you recall? What did you miss?

3:00 Do some fingerprint work. Rub a pencil on a piece of paper until you get a heavily coated area. Wash and dry your hands. Beginning with your pinky, rub your fingertip on the smudge until the skin is covered with graphite. Press a small piece of Scotch tape on your fingertip, press gently, and then tape it to a clean piece of paper. Label each print to indicate which finger it is from. What type of fingerprint do you have? Check http://www.fbi.gov/hq/cjisd/takingfps.html to see the different types.

4:00 Tomorrow you will be talking to the students at a middle school about staying safe on the Internet and being good cybercitizens. Plan a five to 10 minute presentation. Look for good advice at Web sites such as http://tcs.cybertipline.org/knowthedangers.htm or http://www.cybercrime.gov/rules/kidinternet.htm.

5:00 You want to practice your powers of logic and reasoning. After all, sometimes a crime scene, or a mysterious event, doesn't have physical evidence to analyze. Or you don't want to wait for lab results. See how many of the MysteryNet's Kids Mysteries you can solve. Go to http://kids.mysterynet.com. Click on Quick Solve for some short problems, or Solve-It for more complicated ones.

Virtual Apprentice

FBI AGENT: FIELD REPORT

If this is your book, use the space below to jot down a few notes about your Virtual Apprentice experience (or use a blank sheet of paper if this book doesn't belong to you). What did you do? What did you learn? Which activities did you enjoy the most? Don't be stingy with the details!

9:00 WORK OUT: _____

_____

_____

_____

10:00 BLOOD SPATTER EXPERIMENT: _____

_____

_____

_____

11:00 CRACK THE CODE: _____

_____

_____

_____

_____

12:00 LUNCH: _____

_____

1:00 WITNESS INTERVIEW: _____

_____

_____

_____

_____

_____

2:00 OBSERVATION RECALL: _____

_____

_____

_____

_____

_____

3:00 FINGERPRINTING: _____

_____

_____

_____

_____

4:00 CYBER SAFETY PRESENTATION: _____

_____

_____

_____

_____

_____

5:00 SOLVE THE MYSTERY: _____

_____

_____

_____

_____

Count Me In (or Out)

SPECIAL INTEREST OR SPECIAL AGENT?

Any TV show that features an FBI agent in it is automatically on your don't-miss-it list. You can just see yourself spoiling the plans the bad guys are making, rescuing people who are in danger, and bringing the criminals to justice when crimes are committed.

Still want to go for it? Or is the going a little more tough than you imagined?

Find out now. Grab a sheet of paper, a pen or pencil, and see how you respond to these questions. Hold on to your answer sheet; it will be good to look at as you head toward that FBI badge.

If my job required me to move to a different part of the country, I would:

❑ Start packing now. Good thing I don't accumulate a lot of stuff.

❑ Freak out. How can I leave my friends and the room I just decorated?

If I couldn't pass the physical requirements to be on a team I really wanted, I would:

❑ Accept my limitations and look for another type of club or organization.

❑ Work out every day until I could do whatever was needed to make it on the team.

When I have to do a research paper and I can't find any books about my topic in the school library, I:

❑ Tell my teacher that it is an impossible topic and ask her for a new one.

❑ Keep thinking of new places to try for information. There's got to be a way to do this.

The FBI training at Quantico sounds like:

❑ My worst nightmare! Thanks for the warning!

❑ A real challenge, but I know I could succeed if I made my mind up to do it.

Being an FBI Agent

❑   is the perfect career for me because: _____

_____

_____

❑   makes NO sense because: _____

_____

_____

If I were to become an FBI Special Agent, the area I would most like to specialize in is

_____

_____

_____

I love the idea of working for the FBI, but I think I'd prefer to work in one of these support positions: _____

_____

_____

As for a future with the FBI

❑   I'm ready to start now! Here's what I'm planning to do to make it happen:

_____

_____

_____

❑   Forget about it. What I'd really like to do instead is:

_____

_____

_____

APPENDIX

More Resources for Young FBI Agents

BOOKS

Balcavage, Dynise. *The Federal Bureau of Investigation*. Philadelphia: Chelsea House Publishers, 2000.

Graham, Ian. *Crime-Fighting*. Austin, Texas: Raintree Steck-Vaughn, 1995.

January, Brendan. *The FBI*. New York: Franklin Watts, 2002.

Platt, Richard. *Forensics*. Boston: Kingfisher, 2005.

Reeves, Diane Lindsey and Lindsey Clasen. *Career Ideas for Kids Who Like Adventure and Travel*. New York: Facts On File, 2007.

PROFESSIONAL ASSOCIATIONS

FBI Agents Association
P.O. Box 12650
Arlington, Virginia 22219
http://www.fbiaa.org

WEB SITES

Central Intelligence Agency (CIA)
https://www.cia.gov

CIA Museum
https://www.cia.gov/about-cia/cia-museum/index.html

FBI Youth
www.fbi.gov/kids/6th12th/6th12th.htm

Federal Bureau of Investigation
http://www.fbi.gov/

How the FBI Works
http://people.howstuffworks.com/fbi.htm

International Spy Museum
http://www.spymuseum.org

United States Secret Service
http://www.secretservice.gov

US Intelligence and Security Agencies
http://www.fas.org/irp/official.html

INDEX